Harlequin's diamond-patterned costume is well known.
But the earliest drawings of four hundred years ago
   show him wearing a suit with irregular patches,
   roughly sewn on. Only later was it formalized
   into the familiar diamond shapes.
This story about how Harlequin got his patchwork suit
   takes place during the merry holiday of Carnival.
   It is based on an outline found in Larousse's
   Dictionnaire Universel du XIX Siecle, 1865.
Carnival comes just before Lent, a time when people
   give up what they like best. Everyone can have
   their fill of their favorite things at Carnival,
   so that afterwards they won't mind so much going
   without them.
Giving things up is an important part of the story, too.
   For if his friends had not given up a little of
   something that was dear to them, Harlequin would
   never have gotten his costume.

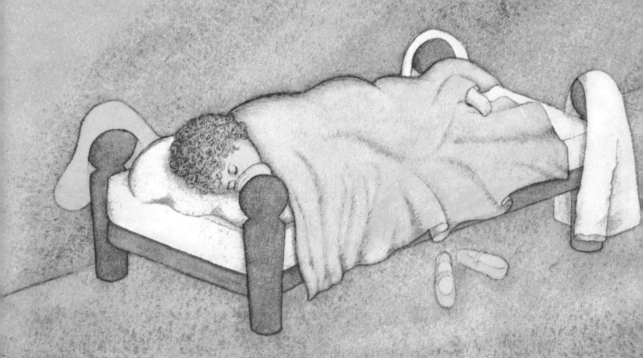

by Remy Charlip & Burton Supree
design & paintings by Remy Charlip

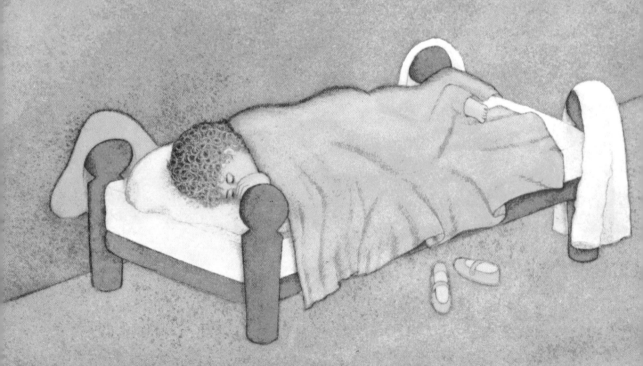

Published by Parents' Magazine Press/New York

HARLEQUIN
and The Gift of Many Colors

Library of Congress Cataloging in Publication Data

Charlip, Remy.
    Harlequin and the gift of many colors.

    SUMMARY: Due to the generosity of his friends, Har-
lequin gets a new patchwork suit for Carnival.
    I. Supree, Burton, joint author. II. Title.
PZZ.C3812Har   [E]   76-136999
ISBN 0-8193-0494-8 ISBN 0-8193-0495-6 (lib. bdg.)

Dedicated to William Burdick and Carmen Fornes

Harlequin awoke.

His room was dark and the stars and the moon were
  still in the sky. It was chilly when he got out of bed,
  so Harlequin wrapped his blanket around him.
  And when he walked to the balcony window, he
  felt as if he were wearing the night.

He saw the shadowy figures of people passing in the
  street below. They had all left home in the dark
  to get to the town square early this morning.

But Harlequin sighed, got back into his warm bed,
  curled up and pulled the covers over his head.

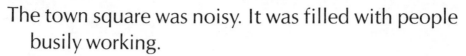

The town square was noisy. It was filled with people
busily working.
They were bringing great trays of cakes,
pies and cookies, and sawing and hammering
wood into little stands where drinks and tasty food
would be sold tonight. They were building booths
for games, too, with prizes if your aim was good or
if you were lucky.

The children were all helping, too, running errands, carrying things, and joking with one another. They could hardly wait for tonight's great Carnival, where there would be candy and ice cream and dancing and singing and laughing friends and, best of all, everyone wearing a splendid new costume!

"But where is Harlequin?" one of the children asked.
Harlequin was usually the first one up and the one
to lead the others on to all sorts of fun.
"I haven't seen him all morning."

"Maybe he was bad and his mother won't let him come out."
"Maybe he's sick. We'd better go see."
And they all ran off to Harlequin's house.

"Harlequin! Harlequin, are you there?"
He appeared at the window wearing his blanket.
"Are you all right?"
"Come on out!"
His friends all started talking at once.
"Harlequin, we peeked into the storeroom. The
    fireworks are all finished."
"My father says I can stay up as late as I want to!"
"Can you smell the chocolate?"
"Hurry, let's get back to the square! I want to
    watch the jugglers practicing."
They were so busy telling Harlequin all the latest
    news that they didn't notice how quiet and
    gloomy he was.
Slowly Harlequin dressed and came down.

Walking back to the square, the children began to
    chatter about the new costumes they would wear for
    the first time tonight. With masks over their faces,
    no one would recognize them. Oh, what tricks
    they could get away with then!
But it was hard not to boast and tease with little
    hints about their costumes.
"Mine is yellow."
"My suit is velvet."
"I've got the biggest green buttons you ever saw!"

"I'm not going to tell you anything about mine, except
that it has fine lace all around."
"Wait till you see mine. It's purple, and it's brocade."
And again they were all talking at once, parading
around in their old clothes, and showing off as if
they were already wearing the new ones.
It was only then that they realized Harlequin had
been silent all this time.
"What are you going to wear tonight, Harlequin?"
They all turned to him.

Harlequin just shrugged his shoulders.
"Oh, Harlequin, you've got to tell. We told you."
"Well," said Harlequin, thinking fast, "I'll wear my
    blanket as a cape."
They thought Harlequin was fooling them as usual.
"Not that old thing!"
"Come on, Harlequin, give us a clue."
"What color is it?"
"What are you going to wear tonight?"
"Nothing," Harlequin replied. "I'm not even coming
    tonight."
And he turned and ran away.

Harlequin not coming? How could that be? How could
   he miss Carnival?
Perhaps he was teasing. He was always playing tricks.
"Wait," one of them said, "I think I know why he's not
   coming tonight. He doesn't have a new costume."
And it was then that they all realized what was the
   matter. Harlequin had nothing to wear because his
   mother was too poor to buy material for a costume.

To think of having a good time without Harlequin
    seemed impossible.
"What can we do?"
"I know! I have an idea. My jacket doesn't need to be
    so long. I can cut some off and give it to Harlequin.
    And if we each give him a piece of cloth,
    then he will have enough for a whole costume."
"Yes! My dress doesn't need to be so long either."
"Good! Let's go and get our cloth and meet in front
    of Harlequin's house."

The sun was directly overhead when all the children met at Harlequin's house. Each one was carrying his gift of cloth.

When Harlequin answered the knock on the door, he was surprised to see all his friends. Then they held out the pieces of cloth and happily pushed them into his hands.

But when the children saw Harlequin's arms filled with
the cut-off bits and scraps, they were dismayed. Each
piece was a different shape and size and color. Some
were smooth, some were shiny, and some were fuzzy.
None of the pieces matched. They looked like a
bunch of rags.

Harlequin politely thanked them, but the children were
afraid they had made matters worse by giving him
such a useless gift.

"I feel so stupid," one of them whispered.

Unhappily they said good-bye and left.

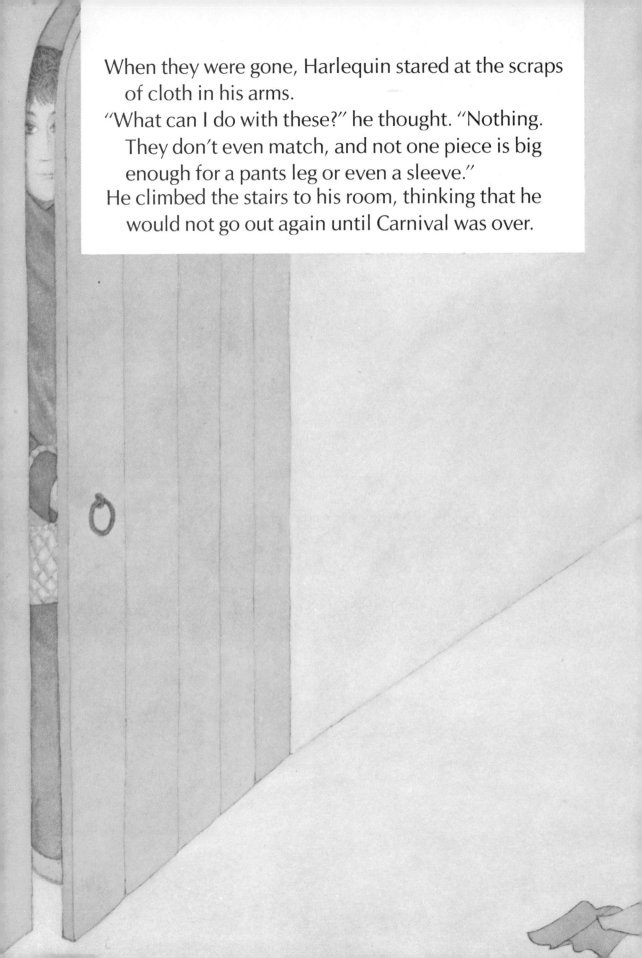

When they were gone, Harlequin stared at the scraps
   of cloth in his arms.
"What can I do with these?" he thought. "Nothing.
   They don't even match, and not one piece is big
   enough for a pants leg or even a sleeve."
He climbed the stairs to his room, thinking that he
   would not go out again until Carnival was over.

But as he tossed the heap of cloth onto the floor,
one piece stuck to his shirt. He looked at it
for a moment. And then he had an idea.

When his mother came home, Harlequin told her all that had happened. Then he told her his idea.

"Do you think if we put all these scraps onto my old
    suit, it would make a good costume?"
His mother looked carefully at the pieces of cloth.
    She turned them over and over in her hands.
    Would it work?
Then she smiled. "I think it would be beautiful,"
    she said.
And they both set to work. Harlequin chose a blue
    piece. Then he pinned a green one next to it.
    He pinned all the pieces where he wanted them,
    and his mother began to sew them on.

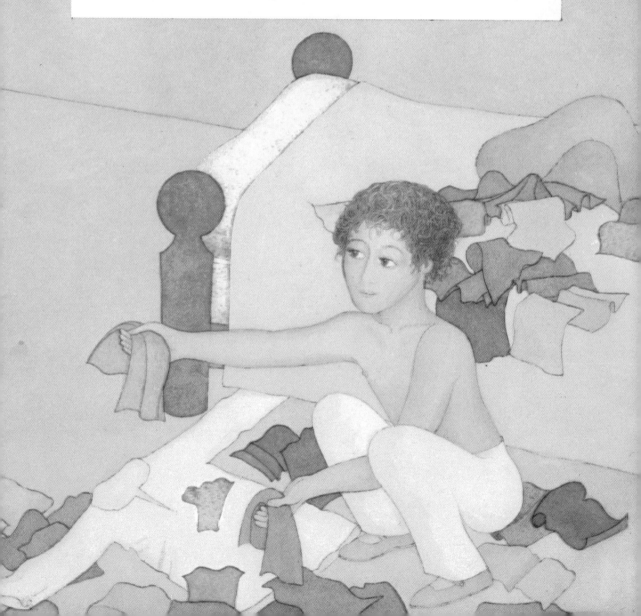

The sewing took a long time. While his mother was sewing the pieces on his old trousers, Harlequin climbed into bed to keep warm. And before he knew it, he had dozed off.

But his mother worked on, worried that she might not be able to finish before nightfall.

"Wake up, Harlequin, it's all finished!"
Moonlight streamed into his room. He heard music and
    shouting in the distance. He blinked his eyes.
    For a moment he didn't know where he was.
Then he realized that he was not dreaming. His mother
    was standing by his bed, smiling and holding up a
    beautiful rainbow-colored suit.

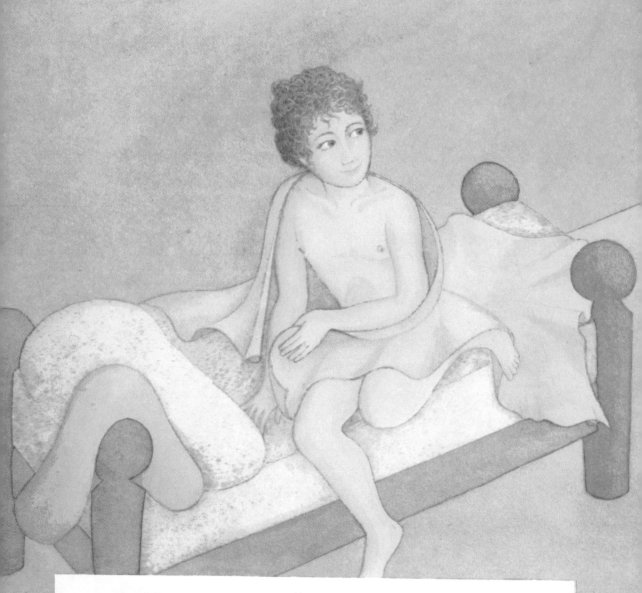

"It's finished!" He threw the covers off and jumped
    out of bed. "Let me put it on!"

"How splendid you look," his mother said proudly.
He spun around and around, as bright as a butterfly.
"Oh, thank you, I love it," Harlequin said as he put
    on his mask and his big hat. "It's wonderful!"
And in a moment he ran off down to the square.

The town square was wild with color and noise. All the world seemed to be dancing and singing there. Tempting smells of broiling meats and sweet pies filled the air. Musicians were playing all the songs everyone liked to hear.

Because it was considered lucky to get the sales started, the first one to come to a booth to buy something did not have to pay. Harlequin's friends had all come early and were running from one booth to another, trying to be first. But they kept looking out for Harlequin, too, hoping that by some miracle their favorite friend might be able to come.

Suddenly a figure appeared in a costume so splendid that everyone stopped what they were doing. The children all crowded around to see.
"What a fantastic costume!"

"I've never seen anything so beautiful!"
"Who is it?"
"Where is he from?"
"Do you know him?"

No one knew.
Whoever it was, he began to leap and dance and turn so joyfully that the crowd laughed and applauded with delight. All the many different colors he wore gleamed and flashed in the light like jewels.

In a flash one of the children recognized a piece of
    his own costume.
"That piece of blue is mine!" he shouted.
"That shiny red stuff is mine!" said another. "That
    must be Harlequin!"

"It *is* Harlequin!"

"Harlequin! Harlequin!" the children cheered, as they dashed through the crowd to greet him. They danced around, hugging him and each other with pleasure.

And Harlequin was the happiest of them all
on this happy night, for he was clothed
in the love of his friends.